P9-DNG-872

To Audri, Elizabeth, and Abby
Magic and peace, and the wish to be wise
May that be what you see in a unicorn's eyes
T. B.

For Paramahansa Yogananda,
my guru of the heart, and for Eve,
who became the heart of Tanisa

G. S.

The Eyes of the Unicorn

BY TERESA BATEMAN

ILLUSTRATED BY GREG SPALENKA

Holiday House / New York

O h, a unicorn's horn
is a marvelous thing.
It can heal and it purifies.
But you'd better beware
for few men will dare
to look in a unicorn's eyes.

The stone walls of the great hall echoed as the nobles gathered for the feast shifted uneasily. The duke glared at the traveling minstrel, and his son, Chris, did the same. Tanisa, the serving girl, sighed.

Tanisa had been the one to open the gate at the minstrel's knock that morning. She had thought it a stroke of good fortune since there were guests to be entertained. The duke, of course, did not listen to a serving maid; but he did listen to his counselor, who listened to the butler, who listened to the cook, who listened, occasionally, to Tanisa. So the minstrel had been hired.

Indeed, at first the minstrel's songs had been merry and beguiling, but this last one left a dissonance that lingered in the air like the cry of a hawk swooping toward its prey.

The platter in Tanisa's hand was slipping. She tried, unsuccessfully, to steady it. The ringing of bronze against stone, when it hit the floor, seemed to clear the air. Tanisa scooped up the platter and fled the room, stopping in the hall to catch her breath.

Someone snickered, and others joined in. Tanisa recognized Chris's laughter. "I'll capture the unicorn, and make a cup from its horn and a rug from its hide," one voice declared.

"No, the unicorn is mine," another replied. "I'll sell its bones to magicians but keep the horn for myself. Ground unicorn horn prolongs life."

"I've heard that artists will sell their souls for brushes made from the hairs of a unicorn's tail," came another voice.

"Just so you're sure there really is a unicorn."

That had sounded like the minstrel.

The duke's voice rumbled out a reply. "How
else would you explain that a stream once
foul and poisoned now runs clear? That
a woodsman, injured by his ax, wakes
to find his leg healed with no sign of
a wound at all? Then there's the early
spring. They say a unicorn always
brings spring with its passing."
There was a murmur of agreement,
then the nobles headed to their
chambers to sharpen swords
and fetch arrows for the hunt ahead.
Tanisa hurried to the kitchen. She waited
for the minstrel to pass through, as was the
custom, to take a bundle of food for the road; but he
never came. Perhaps that was wise, for the duke was
an unforgiving man—giving no quarter to servants nor
sons. Tanisa smiled, then frowned at the thought of Chris.
They had been playmates when they were young, until the
duke found out. Chris had been a sweet boy who wrote wonderful
poetry, but the duke was turning him into a smaller copy of himself.
Now she could hardly see the boy she had known in the eyes of the
young man who sat at the high table that night, laughing with the rest.

She had other things to worry about, however. There was a mountain of dishes to wash. She comforted herself. On the morrow she could rest, for the hunting party would leave early and not return until evening.

Tanisa's one small comfort, however, did not last.

"Tomorrow," the cook informed her, "you will go with the hunters to serve the luncheons. This the duke has commanded."

Tanisa had scarcely closed her eyes when she was being shaken awake. She packed a donkey cart with food and drink. Nobles were riding their fine steeds. Hounds whined their anxiety for the chase.

By the time Tanisa arrived at the meadow, the cry had been given and the hunters were off, seeking the death of a unicorn and their own fame and fortune. Tanisa saw Chris among them, and she felt a wave of disappointment. As a boy he had never even so much as crushed a spider beneath his heel. Now he would kill a unicorn?

She began lunch preparations. The baying of hounds faded away, and birdsong returned to the meadow.

At last everything was ready. Tanisa collapsed beneath a sycamore. "I'll just rest for a bit," she thought, but soon her eyes drifted shut.

Tanisa was never sure, afterward, how much time had passed. She only knew that she drifted up from slumber to feel a heavy weight in her lap.

Forcing her eyes open, she gazed down. Lying by her side was a unicorn. Its head rested gently on her apron; its eyes gazed up into hers.

She looked into the unicorn's eyes and saw there such peace and such love that she wanted nothing more than to spend the rest of her days gazing. Indeed, she might have done just that had she not heard a voice and footsteps drawing near.

"I lost the hunt and my horse," Chris was muttering to himself. "Father will have my head."

Then his voice faltered as he entered the meadow and spied the maid and her companion. Tanisa started to rise and curtsy but could not for the weight in her lap. She caressed the unicorn's head and rubbed her cheek against its golden horn, then smiled up like sunrise, silently inviting Chris to rejoice in the miracle before them.

"The unicorn!" Chris's whisper was harsh. "And I, alone, here to slay it. At last my father will think me worthy to be his heir."

Indeed, the only thing between him and his goal was a small serving maid, and she could hardly count for anything at all.

He raised his bow. Tanisa's eyes widened. Chris hesitated, then readied his arrow to pierce the unicorn's heart.

With a cry, Tanisa flung herself across the unicorn's flank. Her action was so unexpected that Chris accidentally loosed the arrow, and it sped, swift and sure, toward its new target.

The unicorn heaved itself to its feet in a flash, shifting Tanisa so that the arrow only grazed her arm, then stuck quivering in the sycamore tree. But Chris's eyes did not follow the arrow. They widened in horror at the sight of red blood dripping onto the pure white hide of the unicorn.

Tanisa hardly noticed her wound. She faced Chris without the subservience and fear she had learned over the years. She stood, her arm bleeding, and glared.

"What did you plan to do when you killed the unicorn?" she asked.

"Why, keep his horn and sell his hide and bones," Chris replied. He didn't seem to notice he was talking to a mere serving maid. He spoke as when they were children, before they realized they were not equals.

"And when all the unicorns are gone?" Tanisa asked.

"Then the horn and the hide and the bones will be worth even more," Chris replied, sounding like his father.

"How did you know there was a unicorn about?" she asked softly.

"Why, the water was pure and the man was healed and spring came early to the land . . . ," he replied, but his voice trailed off.

"How will you replace that?" Tanisa asked simply as she crumbled to the ground.

Then the unicorn looked directly at Chris and, despite all the warnings he had heard, Chris looked into the unicorn's eyes. And in them he saw himself, cruelly killing an innocent beast that did nothing but good.

The unicorn turned its back to him, offering the perfect target as it extended its horn to gently touch Tanisa's arm. Chris did not take advantage of the chance it offered. Instead he knelt at Tanisa's side, gasping as he watched the flesh knit together again.

Tanisa opened her eyes and saw the unicorn turn and thrust its horn toward Chris's chest. She could see from the expression on the young man's face that he expected a fair return for his arrow. He closed his eyes in acceptance of his fate.

At the last moment the unicorn slowed its thrust and merely touched the top of its golden horn to the center of Chris's chest.

Then Tanisa understood. Chris's heart had been injured over the years as her arm had been injured by the arrow, and his injury was the deeper one.

When Chris opened his eyes again they were filled with the joy she remembered from when they were children. He looked deep into the unicorn's eyes and smiled at what he now saw there.

Suddenly the howling of hounds broke the silence. The hunters were returning to eat. They would be at the clearing within minutes.

Chris bundled some bread and cheese from the tent into one of the duke's linen napkins and thrust the bundle into Tanisa's hands.

"Go. Take the unicorn and flee to the western wilderness. I will send the hunt to the east after lunch with some tale or other."

"Come with us," Tanisa urged.

Chris shook his head. "This land is not safe for a unicorn now," he said sadly. "We will have to clean the water ourselves, heal the sick to the best of our abilities, and accept spring when it comes on its own. But I promise you this: One day I will rule this land, and when I do, I will make it a place where a unicorn may dwell in peace. Then we will have earned the right to have unicorns among us. I will send word when it is safe."

The unicorn at her side, Tanisa walked into the woods. She glanced back only once to see a smile on Chris's face and a look of resolve in his eyes.

As Tanisa and the unicorn melted into the dappled shade of the sycamore trees, she thought she heard the minstrel's song on the breeze. But now there was a new verse to the music:

Oh, a unicorn's horn
is a marvelous thing.
It can soften a heart that cries.
And the legend foretold
that a man who is bold
can be changed
in a unicorn's eyes.

Text copyright © 2007 by Teresa Bateman

Illustrations copyright © 2007 by Greg Spalenka

All Rights Reserved

Printed and Bound in China

The text typeface is Celestia Antiqua.

Creation of the art in this book started with pencil sketches, which were

then digitally scanned. The scanned drawings were integrated with photography,

paint and other collage elements in Photoshop.

www.holidayhouse.com

First Edition

1 3 5 7 9 10 8 6 4 2

Library of Congress Cataloging-in-Publication Data

Bateman, Teresa

The eyes of the unicorn / by Teresa Bateman ; illustrated by Greg Spalenka.— 1st ed.

p. cm.

Summary: A serving girl, disappointed that her childhood friend is becoming a copy
of his proud and unforgiving father, the Duke, helps him to see that the unicorn sought
by the Duke's hunting party is too precious to kill.

ISBN-13: 978-0-8234-1728-5

ISBN-10: 0-8234-1728-X

[1. Unicorns—Fiction. 2. Aristocracy (Social class) —Fiction.]

I. Spalenka, Greg, ill. II. Title.

PZ7.B294435Ey 2003

[Fic]—dc21

2002038716

Designed by Greg Spalenka and Jeff Burne